The Donkey's Story

LOTHROP, LEE & SHEPARD BOOKS • NEW YORK

The Donkey's Story

A Bible Story

RETOLD BY

BARBARA COHEN

ILLUSTRATED BY SUSAN JEANNE COHEN

Library of Congress Cataloging in Publication Data. Cohen, Barbara. The donkey's story. Summary:
A somewhat humorous retelling, featuring Balaam's donkey, of the Bible story in which Balak, king of
Moab, calls upon Balaam, the prophet, to curse the Israelites, but he blesses them instead.
1. Balaam (Biblical figure)—Juvenile literature.   2. Bible stories, English—O.T. Numbers.   [1. Bible
stories—O.T.   2. Balaam, the prophet]   I. Cohen, Susan Jeanne, ill.   II. Title.   BS580.B3C58
1988   222'.14'09505   85-27   ISBN 0-688-04104-3   ISBN 0-688-04105-1 (lib. bdg.)

Let me tell you something. Don't call a dumb person an ass. That's a mistake. Call him a balaam if you want, which is how we donkeys refer to a foolish member of our species. I'll tell you why, in case you don't already know.

Balaam was a human being who lived long ago, with his faithful donkey Sosi, on the banks of the Euphrates River. He had a reputation as a prophet. He believed it himself.

One day a huge delegation came to see him. There must have been thirty, forty men in the crowd, all with long beards and deep, slow voices.

"We are elders of Moab and Midian," they said. "We come to you from the mighty ruler Balak, king of Moab."

"A great people has settled in the desert next to Moab," the elders explained. "There are so many of them that you can't see the earth beneath their camp. The mighty Balak will do battle against them. But before he fights them, he wants you to curse them. If you curse them, he will surely defeat them, and drive them out of the land. For Balak knows that Balaam is a powerful prophet. He whom Balaam blesses is blessed, and he whom Balaam curses is cursed."

Of course Balaam was flattered. But he knew where his power really came from. So he said, "Spend the night here. I'll answer you in the morning as God instructs me."

In the night, God came to Balaam and said, "Don't go with those men. You mustn't curse the people Balak wants you to curse, for they are blessed."

In the morning, Balaam said to the elders of Moab and Midian, "Go on home. The Lord God won't let me come with you."

They left, but in a few weeks even more of them were back again, with another message from King Balak: "I will give Balaam anything he wants if he will curse these people for me."

"If Balak gave me his own house full of silver and gold, I couldn't go against the word of the Lord my God," Balaam replied. "But stay the night. Perhaps the Lord will say something else to me."

Balaam dreamt of jewels and great honors, and he thought he heard God's voice say to him, "You may go with those men."

In the morning Balaam saddled old Sosi and rode
off with the princes of Moab, who were mounted on
their horses and camels.

They were far ahead of him when suddenly, for no
reason that Balaam could see, old Sosi swerved from
the road and went off into the fields. "Stupid beast!"
Balaam cried. "Get back on the road!" And he beat
her with his stick.

But Sosi knew that God's angel stood in the way.
Sosi pressed herself against the wall that bordered the
lane, accidentally squeezing Balaam's foot so hard
against the stones that he uttered a yelp and beat her
again until he raised welts on her weathered hide.

The angel stepped toward Sosi. Now the angel
stood in a place so narrow there was no room for Sosi
to move, to the right or to the left. On the spot, she
folded her legs beneath her and lay down. This time
Balaam beat her so hard that God took pity on her
and opened her mouth.

"What have I done to you, silly man?" Sosi demanded. "What have I done to you that you should beat me cruelly three times in a row?"

"You've made an ass of *me*," Balaam retorted. "If I had a sword, I'd kill you!"

"Look," said Sosi, "who are you talking to here? You're talking to your faithful old Sosi. You've ridden me every day since I was big enough to carry you. Did I ever do anything like this to you before?"

"No," Balaam admitted.

"Then look behind you," said Sosi.

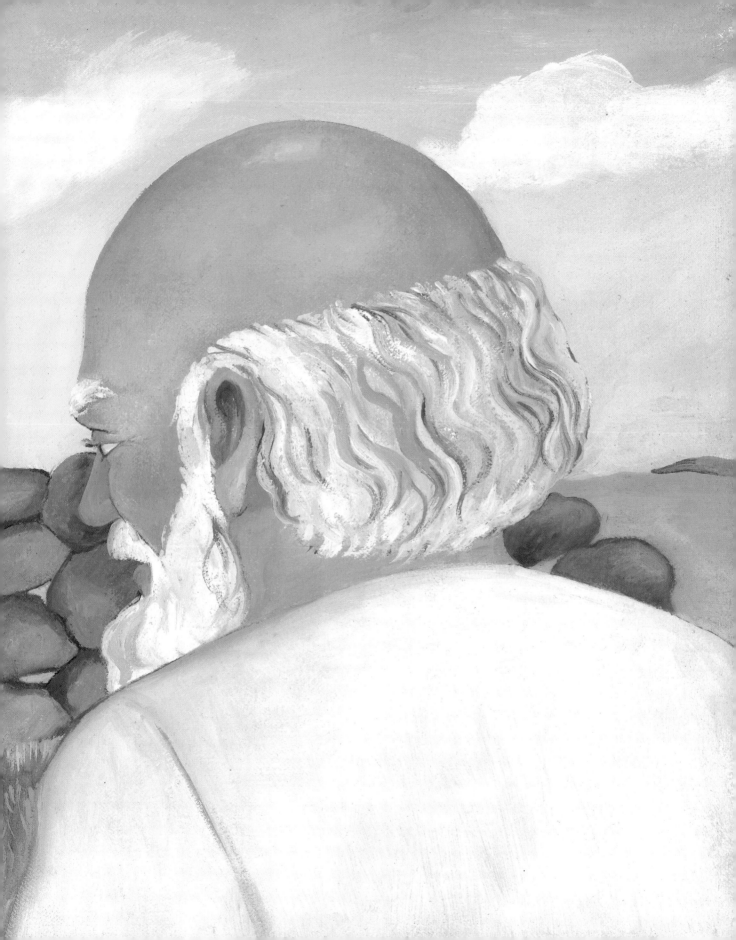

Balaam looked, and now he was able to see. He saw the angel of God, standing in the way, his drawn sword in his hand. Balaam bowed so low that his nose touched the ground.

"Why have you beaten your donkey three times?" the angel scolded. "It's me you should be mad at. I stand here in your way because God doesn't like what you're doing. Sosi shied three times because she saw me. Believe me, if she'd run over me, it's you I'd have killed, not her."

"I made a mistake," Balaam apologized. "If God doesn't approve of this trip, I'll turn back."

"No, it's all right," the angel said. "Keep going. But you will say nothing except the words God puts in your mouth."

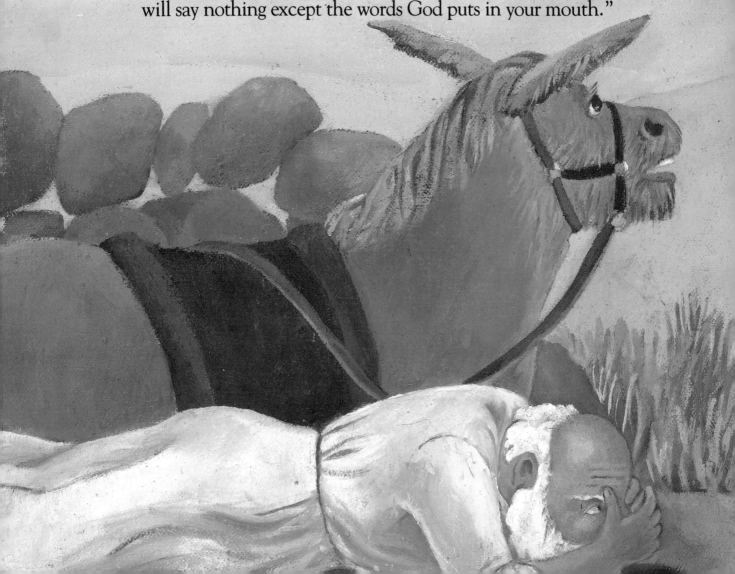

Meanwhile, King Balak had come out to meet
Balaam. He made a great feast of sheep and oxen for
the prophet and all the other important men.
Afterward, he led Balaam and Sosi to the top of a hill.
"Look," he said. "You can see my enemies from here."

Sosi gazed out at the tents of the Israelites filling the
valley.

"Build me seven altars," said Balaam, "and bring me seven young bulls and seven rams." When this was done, Balaam and Balak offered up a bull and a ram on each altar.

"Now," said Balaam, "you stay here with your offerings. I'll go off alone, and whatever God says to me, I'll tell you."

Balaam went into the wilderness, riding Sosi. "Oh, God," Balaam said, "I have set up seven altars and offered you a bull and a ram on each one."

"Well," said God, "return to Balak and tell him what I tell you to tell him."

Balaam and Sosi returned to the king, and Balaam spoke the words that God had put into his mouth.

Balak brought me here from my country.
Moab's king brought me here from the hills of the East.
"Curse Jacob for me," he said.
"Come, tell Israel's doom."
How can I damn those whom God has not damned?
How can I doom when the Lord has not doomed?
Who can bewitch Jacob?
Who can cast a spell on Israel?
May I die the death of the upright.
May my fate be like theirs!

Balak was furious. "What have you done to me?" he exclaimed. "Here I brought you to damn my enemies, and instead you've blessed them!"

"Oh, dear," said Balaam. "I can only repeat the words the Lord puts in my mouth."

"Let's try again," Balak suggested. "We'll go to another place, from where you can see more of them. You can damn them for me from there."

Sosi shook her head, but Balaam ignored her. He went with Balak to another hilltop. Seven more altars were built, and Balaam and Balak offered up a ram and a bull on each altar.

Then Balaam left Balak standing beside his offerings, and rode Sosi into the wilderness, where God said to him, "Well, go back and say the words that I tell you."

So Balaam and Sosi returned to Balak. "What did the Lord say?" Balak asked.

And Balaam replied:

Get up, Balak, and pay attention.
Listen to me, son of Zippor.
God doesn't change his mind, as people do.
Would He say something and not do it?
Would He make a promise and not keep it?
My message was to bless.
When He blesses I cannot curse.

"All right, all right," Balak interrupted, "so don't curse them. But you don't have to bless them either."

"I told you," Balaam reminded him. "What the Lord says, I must do."

"Let's try again," Balak suggested.

Sosi shook her head, but Balaam followed Balak to another high place. Again seven altars were built, and Balak and Balaam offered up a bull and a ram on each one.

Balaam and Sosi stood on the hilltop. Sosi waved her tail. Balaam lifted his arms and opened his mouth. Out came the words that God told him to say:

How goodly are your tents, O Jacob,
Your dwelling places, O Israel!
Like groves of palm trees that stretch out,
Like gardens beside a river,
Like sweet blossoms planted by the Lord,
Like cedar trees beside the water;
Their branches drip with droplets,
Their roots have all the water that they need.
Their king shall rise up above other kings,
Their kingdom shall be lifted high.

Balak clapped his hands together. "I called you to damn my enemies, and instead you've blessed them three times! Go home! I was going to give you pots full of gold and silver, but your God has seen to it that you won't get a single birdseed."

"Listen," Balaam reminded him, "I told your messengers that even if you gave me your house full of silver and gold, what the Lord says, that I must say."

Sosi brayed her agreement.

"Before I go back to my own people," Balaam added, "I have something else to tell you."

What I see for Israel is not yet.
What I behold will not come soon.
A star rises from Jacob,
A bright light comes forth from Israel,
It smashes the brow of Moab.
But Israel is triumphant.
Who can survive, except God has willed it?

Sosi shook her bridle and stirrups. Then she and Balaam set out on their journey home. Sosi never spoke another word to a human being as long as she lived, and neither has any donkey since.

After all, what's the use?

Notes on *The Donkey's Story*

The story of Balaam appears in the fourth book of the
Bible, Numbers, Chapters 23-24. My version of the tale owes
much to the most recent Jewish Publication Society
translation, prepared by a committee headed by Dr. Harry
Orlinsky, and to the commentary of Robert Alter in *The Art of
Biblical Narrative* (Basic Books, 1981).

There is much in the story of Balaam and Balak that is
deeply serious, but the story is also humorous. Many funny
stories are also deeply serious. One of the reasons this story
appealed to me for retelling was that we are not accustomed to
thinking of a Bible story as humorous. It is obvious, though,
that the original teller of the tale intended it to be funny.
Anyone who does not smile at the idea of Balaam's ass lying
down in the middle of a field and giving Balaam what for is
missing one point of the story.

Balaam is not an heroic figure. He is greedy, duplicitous,
and puffed up with his own importance. But if God spoke only
through perfect people, who would ever hear His voice?
Though flawed, like the rest of us, Balaam proves himself
capable of rising to the occasion—which, one can hope, is
also like the rest of us.

BARBARA COHEN